Paul Bourget

Cosmopolis
Volume III

Paul Bourget

Cosmopolis
Volume III

1st Edition | ISBN: 978-3-73408-659-5

Place of Publication: Frankfurt am Main, Germany

Year of Publication: 2019

Outlook Verlag GmbH, Germany.

COSMOPOLIS

By PAUL BOURGET

BOOK 3.

CHAPTER VII

A LITTLE RELATIVE OF IAGO

The remorse which Montfanon expressed so naively, once acknowledged to himself, increased rapidly in the honest man's heart. He had reason to say from the beginning that the affair looked bad. A quarrel, together with assault, or an attempt at assault, would not be easily set right. It required a diplomatic miracle. The slightest lack of self-possession on the part of the seconds is equivalent to a catastrophe. As happens in such circumstances, events are hurried, and the pessimistic anticipations of the irritable Marquis were verified almost as soon as he uttered them. Dorsenne and he had barely left the Palais Savorelli when Gorka arrived. The energy with which he repulsed the proposition of an arrangement which would admit of excuses on his part, served prudent Hafner, and the not less prudent Ardea, as a signal for withdrawal. It was too evident to the two men that no reconciliation would result from a collision of such a madman with a personage so difficult as the most authorized of Florent's proxies had shown himself to be. They then asked Gorka to relieve them from their duty. They had too plausible an excuse in Fanny's betrothal for Boleslas to refuse to release them. That retirement was a second catastrophe. In his impatience to find other seconds who would be firm, Gorka hastened to the Cercle de la Chasse. Chance willed that he should meet with two of his comrades—a Marquis Cibo, Roman, and a Prince Pietrapertoso, Neapolitan, who were assuredly the best he could have chosen to hasten the simplest affair to its worst consequences.

Those two young men of the best Italian families, both very intelligent, very loyal and very good, belonged to that particular class which is to be met with in Vienna, Madrid, St. Petersburg, as in Milan and in Rome, of foreign club-men hypnotized by Paris. And what a Paris! That of showy and noisy fetes, that which passes the morning in practising the sports in fashion, the afternoons in racing, in frequenting fencing- schools, the evening at the theatre and the night at the gaming-table! That Paris which emigrates by turns, according to the season, to Monte Carlo for the 'Tir aux Pigeons', to Deauville for the race week, to Aix- les-Bains for the baccarat season; that Paris which has its own customs, its own language, its own history, even its own cosmopolitanism, for it exercises over certain minds, throughout Europe, so despotic a rule that Cibo, for example, and his friend Pietrapertoso never opened a French journal that was not Parisian.

2

They sought the short paragraphs in which were related, in detail, the doings of the demi-monde, the last supper given by some well-known viveur, the details of some large party in such and such a fashionable club, the result of a shooting match, or of a fencing match between celebrated fencers! There were between them subjects of conversation of which they never wearied; to know if spirituelle Gladys Harvey was more elegant than Leona d'Astri, if Machault made "counters" as rapid as those of General Garnier, if little Lautrec would adhere or would not adhere to the game he was playing. Imprisoned in Rome by the scantiness of their means, and also by the wishes, the one of his uncle, the other of his grandfather, whose heirs they were, their entire year was summed up in the months which they spent at Nice in the winter, and in the trip they took to Paris at the time of the Grand Prix for six weeks. Jealous one of the other, with the most comical rivalry, of the least occurrence at the 'Cercle des Champs-Elysees' or of the Rue Royale in the Eternal City, they affected, in the presence of their colleagues of la chasse, the impassive manner of augurs when the telegraph brought them the news of some Parisian scandal. That inoffensive mania which had made of stout, ruddy Cibo, and of thin, pale Pietrapertoso two delightful studies for Dorsenne during his Roman winter, made of them terrible proxies in the service of Gorka's vengeance.

With what joy and what gravity they accepted that mission all those who have studied swordsmen will understand after this simple sketch, and with what promptness they presented themselves to confer at nine o'clock in the morning with their client's adversary! In short, at half-past twelve the duel was arranged in its slightest detail. The energy employed by Montfanon had only ended in somewhat tempering the conditions—four balls to be exchanged at twenty-five paces at the word of command. The duel was fixed for the following morning, in the inclosure which Cibo owned, with an inn adjoining, not very far distant from the classical tomb of Cecilia Metella. To obtain that distance and the use of new weapons it required the prestige with which the Marquis suddenly clothed himself in the eyes of Gorka's seconds by pronouncing the name, still legendary in the provinces and to the foreigner, of Gramont-Caderousse—'Sic transit gloria mundi'! On leaving that rendezvous the excellent man really had tears in his eyes.

"It is my fault," he moaned, "it is my fault. With that Hafner we should have obtained such a fine official plan by mixing in a little of ours. He offered it to us himself.... Brave Chapron! It is I who have brought him into this dilemma! .... I owe it to him not to abandon him, but to follow him to the end.... Here I shall be assisting at a duel, at my age!.... Did you see how those young snobs lowered their voices when I mentioned my encounter with poor Caderousse? .... Fifty-two years and a month, and not to know yet how to conduct one's self! Let us go to the Rue Leopardi. I wish to ask pardon of our client, and to give him some advice. We will take him to one of my old friends who has a garden near the Villa Pamphili, very secluded. We will spend the rest of the afternoon practising…. Ah! Accursed choler! Yes, it would have been so simple to accept the other's plan yesterday. By the exchange of two or three words, I am sure it could have been arranged."

"Console yourself, Marquis," replied Florent, when the unhappy nobleman had described to him the deplorable result of his negotiations. "I like that better. Monsieur Gorka needs correction. I have only one regret, that of not having given it to him more thoroughly…. Since I shall have to fight a duel, I would at least have had my money's worth!"

"And you have never used a pistol?" asked Montfanon.

"Bah! I have hunted a great deal and I believe I can shoot."

"That is like night and day," interrupted the Marquis. "Hold yourself in readiness. At three o'clock come for me and I will give you a lesson. And remember there is a merciful God for the brave!"

Although Florent deserved praise for the cheerfulness of which his reply was proof, the first moments which he spent alone after the departure of his two witnesses were very painful.

That which Chapron experienced during those few moments was simply very natural anxiety, the enervation caused by looking at the clock, and saying:

"In twenty-four hours the hand will be on this point of the dial. And shall I still be living?"…. He was, however, manly, and knew how to control himself. He struggled against the feeling of weakness, and, while awaiting the time to rejoin his friends, he resolved to write his last wishes. For years his intention had been to leave his entire fortune to his brother-in-law. He, therefore, made a rough draft of his will in that sense, with a pen at first rather unsteady, then quite firm. His will completed, he had courage enough to write two letters, addressed the one to that brother-in-law, the other to his sister. When he had finished his work the hands of the clock pointed to ten minutes of three.

"Still seventeen hours and a half to wait," said he, "but I think I have conquered my nerves. A short walk, too, will benefit me."

So he decided to go on foot to the rendezvous named by Montfanon. He carefully locked the three envelopes in the drawer of his desk. He saw, on passing, that Lincoln was not in his studio. He asked the footman if Madame Maitland was at home. The reply received was that she was dressing, and that she had ordered her carriage for three o'clock.

4

"Good," said he, "neither of them will have the slightest suspicion; I am saved."

How astonished he would have been could he, while walking leisurely toward his destination, have returned in thought to the smoking-room he had just left! He would have seen a woman glide noiselessly through the open door, with the precaution of a malefactor! He would have seen her examine, without disarranging, all the papers on the table. She frowned on seeing Dorsenne's and the Marquis's cards. She took from the blotting-case some loose leaves and held them in front of the glass, trying to read there the imprint left upon them. He would have seen finally the woman draw from her pocket a bunch of keys. She inserted one of them in the lock of the drawer which Florent had so carefully turned, and took from that drawer the three unsealed envelopes he had placed within it. And the woman who thus read, with a face contracted by anguish, the papers discovered in such a manner, thanks to a ruse the abominable indelicacy of which gave proof of shameful habits of espionage, was his own sister, the Lydia whom he believed so gentle and so simple, to whom he had penned an adieu so tender in case he should be killed—the Lydia who would have terrified him had he seen her thus, with passion distorting the face which was considered insignificant! She herself, the audacious spy, trembled as if she would fall, her eyes dilated, her bosom heaved, her teeth chattered, so greatly was she unnerved by what she had discovered, by the terrible consequences which she had brought about.

Had she not written the anonymous letters to Gorka, denouncing to him the intrigue between Maitland and Madame Steno? Was it not she who had chosen, the better to poison those terrible letters, phrases the most likely to strike the betrayed lover in the most sensitive part of his 'amour propre'? Was it not she who had hastened the return of the jealous man with the certain hope of drawing thus a tragical vengeance upon the hated heads of her husband and the Venetian? That vengeance, indeed, had broken. But upon whom? Upon the only person Lydia loved in the world, upon the brother whom she saw endangered through her fault; and that thought was to her so overwhelming that she sank into the armchair in which Florent had been seated fifteen minutes before, repeating, with an accent of despair: "He is going to fight a duel. He is going to fight instead of the other!"

All the moral history of that obscure and violent soul was summed up in the cry in which passionate anxiety for her brother was coupled with a fierce hatred of her husband. That hatred was the result of a youth and a childhood without the story of which a duplicity so criminal in a being so young would be unintelligible. That youth and that childhood had presaged what Lydia would one day be. But who was there to train the nature in which the heredity of an oppressed race manifested itself, as has been already remarked, by the two most detestable characteristics— hypocrisy and perfidy? Who, moreover, observes in children the truth, as much neglected in practise as it is common in theory, that the defects of the tenth year become vices in the thirtieth? When quite a child Lydia invented falsehoods as naturally as her brother spoke the truth…. Whosoever observed her would have perceived that those lies were all told to paint herself in a favorable light. The germ, too, of another defect was springing up within her—a jealousy instinctive, irrational, almost wicked. She could not see a new plaything in Florent's hands without sulking immediately. She could not bear to see her brother embrace her father without casting herself between them, nor could she see him amuse himself with other comrades.

Had Napoleon Chapron been interested in the study of character as deeply as he was in his cotton and his sugarcane, he would have perceived, with affright, the early traces of a sinful nature. But, on that point, like his son, he was one of those trustful men who did not judge when they loved. Moreover, Lydia and Florent, to his wounded sensibility of a demi-pariah, formed the only pleasant corner in his life—were the fresh and youthful comforters of his widowerhood and of his misanthropy. He cherished them with the idolatry which all great workers entertain for their children, which is one of the most dangerous forms of paternal tenderness; Lydia's incipient vices were to the planter delightful fancies! Did she lie? The excellent man exclaimed: What an imagination she has! Was she jealous? He would sigh, pressing to his broad breast the tiny form: How sensitive she is!…. The result of that selfish blindness—for to love children thus is to love them for one's self and not for them—was that the girl, at the time of her entrance at Roehampton, was spoiled in the essential traits of her character. But she was so pretty, she owed to the singular mixture of three races an originality of grace so seductive that only the keen glance of a governess of genius could have discerned, beneath that exquisite exterior, the already marked lines of her character. Such governesses are rare, still more so at convents than elsewhere. There was none at Roehampton when Lydia entered that pious haven which was to prove fatal to her, for a reason precisely contrary to that which transformed for Florent the lawns of peaceful Beaumont into a radiant paradise of friendship.

Among the pupils with whom Lydia was to be educated were four young girls from Philadelphia, older than the newcomer by two years, and who, also, had left America for the first time. They brought with them the unconquerable aversion to negro blood and that wonderful keenness in discovering it, even in the most infinitesimal degree, which distinguishes real Yankees. Little Lydia Chapron, having been entered as French, they at first hesitated in the face of a suspicion speedily converted into a certainty and that certainty into an

6

aversion, which they could not conceal. They would not have been children had they not been unfeeling. They, therefore, began to offer poor Lydia petty affronts. Convents and colleges resemble other society. There, too, unjust contempt is like that "ferret of the woods," which runs from hand to hand and which always returns to its point of setting out. All the scornful are themselves scorned by some one—a merited punishment, which does not correct our pride any more than the other punishments which abound in life cure our other faults. Lydia's persecutors were themselves the objects of outrages practised by their comrades born in England, on account of certain peculiarities in their language and for the nasal quality of their voices. The drama was limited, as we can imagine, to a series of insignificant episodes and of which the superintendents only surprised a demi-echo.

Children nurse passions as strong as ours, but so much interrupted by playfulness that it is impossible to measure their exact strength. Lydia's 'amour propre' was wounded in an incurable manner by that revelation of her own peculiarity. Certain incidents of her American life recurred to her, which she comprehended more clearly. She recalled the portrait of her grandmother, the complexion, the hands, the hair of her father, and she experienced that shame of her birth and of her family much more common with children than our optimism imagines. Parents of humble origin give their sons a liberal education, expose them to the demoralization which it brings with it in their positions, and what social hatreds date from the moment when the boy of twelve blushes in secret at the condition of his relatives! With Lydia, so instinctively jealous and untruthful, those first wounds induced falsehood and jealousy. The slightest superiority even, noticed in one of her companions, became to her a cause for suffering, and she undertook to compensate by personal triumphs the difference of blood, which, once discovered, wounds a vain nature. In order to assure herself those triumphs she tried to win all the persons who approached her, mistresses and comrades, and she began to practise that continued comedy of attitude and of sentiment to which the fatal desire to please, so quickly leads- that charming and dangerous tendency which borders much less on goodness than falseness. At eighteen, submitted to a sort of continual cabotinage, Lydia was, beneath the most attractive exterior, a being profoundly, though unconsciously, wicked, capable of very little affection—she loved no one truly but her brother—open to the invasion of the passions of hatred which are the natural products of proud and false minds. It was one of these passions, the most fatal of all, which marriage was to develop within her—envy.

That hideous vice, one of those which govern the world, has been so little studied by moralists, as all too dishonorable for the heart of man, no doubt, that this statement may appear improbable. Madame Maitland, for years, had been envious of her husband, but envious as one of the rivals of an artist would be, envious as one pretty woman is of another, as one banker is of his opponent, as a politician of his adversary, with the fierce, implacable envy which writhes with physical pain in the face of success, which is transported with a sensual joy in the face of disaster. It is a great mistake to limit the ravages of that guilty passion to the domain of professional emulation. When it is deep, it does not alone attack the qualities of the person, but the person himself, and it was thus that Lydia envied Lincoln. Perhaps the analysis of this sentiment, very subtle in its ugliness, will explain to some a few of the antipathies against which they have struck in their relatives. For it is not only between husband and wife that these unavowed envies are met, it is between lover and mistress, friend and friend, brother and brother, sometimes, alas, father and son, mother and daughter! Lydia had married Lincoln Maitland partly out of obedience to her brother's wishes, partly from vanity, because the young man was an American, and because it was a sort of victory over the prejudices of race, of which she thought constantly, but of which she never spoke.

It required only three months of married life to perceive that Maitland could not forgive himself for that marriage. Although he affected to scorn his compatriots, and although at heart he did not share any of the views of the country in which he had not set foot since his fifth year, he could not hear remarks made in New York upon that marriage without a pang. He disliked Lydia for the humiliation, and she felt it. The birth of a child would no doubt have modified that feeling, and, if it would not have removed it, would at least have softened the embittered heart of the young wife. But no child was born to them. They had not returned from their wedding tour, upon which Florent accompanied them, before their lives rolled along in that silence which forms the base of all those households in which husband and wife, according to a simple and grand expression of the people, do not live heart against heart.

After the journey through Spain, which should have been one continued enchantment, the wife became jealous of the evident preference which Florent showed for Maitland. For the first time she perceived the hold which that impassioned friendship had taken upon her brother's heart. He loved her, too, but with a secondary love. The comparison annoyed her daily, hourly, and it did not fail to become a real wound. Returned to Paris, where they spent almost three years, that wound was increased by the sole fact that the puissant individuality of the painter speedily relegated to the shade the individuality of his wife, simply, almost mechanically, like a large tree which pushes a smaller one into the background. The composite society of artists, amateurs, and writers who visited Lincoln came there only for him. The house they had rented was rented only for him. The journeys they made were for him. In short, Lydia was borne away, like Florent, in the orbit of the most despotic force in the world—that of a celebrated talent. An entire book would be required to paint in their daily truth the continued humiliations which brought the young wife to detest that talent and that celebrity with as much ardor as Florent worshipped them. She remained, however, an honest woman, in the sense in which the word is construed by the world, which sums up woman's entire dishonor in errors of love.

But within Lydia's breast grew a rooted aversion toward Lincoln. She detested him for the pure blood which made of that large, fair, and robust man so admirable a type of Anglo-Saxon beauty, by the side of her, so thin, so insignificant indeed, in spite of the grace of her pretty, dark face. She detested him for his taste, for the original elegance with which he understood how to adorn the places in which he lived, while she maintained within her a barbarous lack of taste for the least arrangement of materials and of colors. When she was forced to acknowledge progress in the painter, bitter hatred entered her heart. When he lamented over his work, and when she saw him a prey to the dolorous anxiety of an artist who doubts himself, she experienced a profound joy, marred only by the evident sadness into which Lincoln's struggles plunged Florent. Never had she met the eyes of Chapron fixed upon Maitland with that look of a faithful dog which rejoices in the joy of its master, or which suffers in his sadness, without enduring, like Alba Steno, the sensation of a "needle in the heart."

The idolatrous worship of her brother for the painter caused her to suffer still more as she comprehended, with the infallible perspicacity of antipathy, the immense dupery. She read the very depths of the souls of the two old comrades of Beaumont. She knew that in that friendship, as is almost always the case, one alone gave all to receive in exchange only the most brutal recognition, that with which a huntsman or a master gratifies a faithful dog! As for enlightening Florent with regard to Lincoln's character, she had vainly tried to do so by those fine and perfidious insinuations in which women excel. She only recognized her impotence, and myriads of hateful impressions were thus accumulated in her heart, to be summed up in one of those frenzies of taciturn rancor which bursts on the first opportunity with terrifying energy. Crime itself has its laws of development. Between the pretty little girl who wept on seeing a new toy in her brother's hand and the Lydia Maitland, forcer of locks, author of anonymous letters, driven by the thirst for vengeance, even to villainy, no dramatic revolution of character had taken place. The logical succession of days had sufficed.

The occasion to gratify that deep and mortal longing to touch Lincoln on

9

some point truly sensitive, how often Lydia had sought it in vain, before Madame Steno obtained an ascendancy over the painter. She had been reduced by it to those meannesses of feminine animosity to manage, as if accidentally, that her husband might read all the disagreeable articles written about his paintings, innocently to praise before him the rivals who had given him offense, to repeat to him with an air of embarrassment the slightest criticisms pronounced on one of his exhibits—all the unpleasantnesses which had the result of irritating Florent, above all, for Maitland was one of those artists too well satisfied with the results of his own work for the opinion of others to annoy him very much. On the other hand, before the passion for the dogaresse had possessed him, he had never loved. Many painters are thus, satisfying with magnificent models an impetuosity of temperament which does not mount from the senses to the heart. Accustomed to regard the human form from a certain point, they find in beauty, which would appear to us simply animal, principles of plastic emotion which at times suffice for their amorous requirements. They are only more deeply touched by it, when to that rather coarse intoxication is joined, in the woman who inspires them, the refined graces of mind, the delicacy of elegance and the subtleties of sentiment.

Such was Madame Steno, who at once inspired the painter with a passion as complete as a first love. It was really such. The Countess, who was possessed of the penetration of voluptuousness, was not mistaken there. Lydia, who was possessed of the penetration of hatred, was not mistaken either. She knew from the first day how matters stood in the beginning, because she was as observing as she was dissimulating; then, thanks to means less hypothetic, she had always had the habit of making those abominable inquiries which are natural, we venture to avow, to nine women out of ten! And how many men are women, too, on this point, as said the fabulist. At school Lydia was one of those who ascended to the dormitory, or who reentered the study to rummage in the cupboards and open trunks of her companions. When mature, never had a sealed letter passed through her hands without her having ingeniously managed to read through the envelope, or at least to guess from the postmark, the seal, the handwriting of the address, who was the author of it. The instinct of curiosity was so strong that she could not refrain, at a telegraph office, from glancing over the shoulders of the persons before her, to learn the contents of their despatches. She never had her hair dressed or made her toilette without minutely questioning her maid as to the goings-on in the pantry and the antechamber. It was through a story of that kind that she learned the altercation between Florent and Gorka in the vestibule, which proves, between parentheses, that these espionages by the aid of servants are often efficacious. But they reveal a native baseness, which will not recoil before any piece of villainy.

When Madame Maitland suspected the liaison of Madame Steno and her husband, she no more hesitated to open the latter's secretary than she later hesitated to open the desk of her brother. The correspondence which she read in that way was of a nature which exasperated her desire for vengeance almost to frenzy. For not only did she acquire the evidence of a happiness shared by them which humiliated in her the woman barren in all senses of the word, a stranger to voluptuousness as well as to maternity, but she gathered from it numerous proofs that the Countess cherished, with regard to her, a scorn of race as absolute as if Venice had been a city of the United States.... That part of the Adriatic abounds in prejudices of blood, as do all countries which serve as confluents for every nation. It is sufficient to convince one's self of it, to have heard a Venetian treat of the Slavs as 'Cziavoni', and the Levantines as 'Gregugni'.

Madame Steno, in those letters she had written with all the familiarity and all the liberty of passion, never called Lydia anything but La Morettina, and by a very strange illogicalness never was the name of the brother of La Morettina mentioned without a formula of friendship. As the mistress treated Florent in that manner, it must be that she apprehended no hostility on the part of her lover's brother-in-law. Lydia understood it only too well, as well as the fresh proof of Florent's sentiments for Lincoln. Once more he gave precedence to the friend over the sister, and on what an occasion! The most secret wounds in her inmost being bled as she read. The success of Alba's portrait, which promised to be a masterpiece, ended by precipitating her into a fierce and abominable action. She resolved to denounce Madame Steno's new love to the betrayed lover, and she wrote the twelve letters, wisely calculated and graduated, which had indeed determined Gorka's return. His return had even been delayed too long to suit the relative of Iago, who had decided to aim at Madame Steno through Alba by a still more criminal denunciation. Lydia was in that state of exasperation in which the vilest weapons seem the best, and she included innocent Alba in her hatred for Maitland, on account of the portrait, a turn of sentiment which will show that it was envy by which that soul was poisoned above all. Ah, what bitter delight the simultaneous success of that double infamy had procured for her! What savage joy, mingled with bitterness and ecstacy, had been hers the day before, on witnessing the nervousness of poor Alba and the suppressed fury of Boleslas!

In her mind she had seen Maitland provoked by the rival whom she knew to be as adroit with the sword as with the pistol. She would not have been the great-grandchild of a slave of Louisiana, if she had not combined with the natural energy of her hatreds a considerable amount of superstition. A fortune-

11

teller had once foretold, from the lines in her palm, that she would cause the violent death of some person. "It will be he," she had thought, glancing at her husband with a horrible tremor of hope…. And now she had the proof, the indisputable proof, that her plot for vengeance was to terminate in the danger of another. Of what other?

The letter and will made by Florent disclosed to her the threat of a fatal duel suspended over the head which was the dearest to her. So she had driven to a tragical encounter the only being whom she loved…. The disappointment of the heart in which palpitated the wild energies of a bestial atavism was so sudden, so acute, so dolorous, that she uttered an inarticulate cry, leaning upon her brother's desk, and, in the face of those sheets of paper which had revealed so much, she repeated:

"He is going to fight a duel! He!…. And I am the cause!"…. Then, returning the letters and the will to the drawer, she closed it and rose, saying aloud:

"No. It shall not be. I will prevent it, if I have to cast myself between them. I do not wish it! I do not wish it!"

It was easy to utter such words. But the execution of them was less easy. Lydia knew it, for she had no sooner uttered that vow than she wrung her hands in despair—those weak hands which Madame Steno compared in one of her letters to the paws of a monkey, the fingers were so supple and so long —and she uttered this despairing cry: "But how?"…. which so many criminals have uttered before the issue, unexpected and fatal to them, of their shrewdest calculations. The poet has sung it in the words which relate the story of all our faults, great and small:

"The gods are just, and of our pleasant vices
    Make instruments to plague us."

It is necessary that the belief in the equity of an incomprehensible judge be well grounded in us, for the strongest minds are struck by a sinister apprehension when they have to brave the chance of a misfortune absolutely merited. The remembrance of the soothsayer's prediction suddenly occurred to Lydia. She uttered another cry, rubbing her hands like a somnambulist. She saw her brother's blood flowing…. No, the duel should not take place! But how to prevent it? How-how? she repeated. Florent was not at home. She could, therefore, not implore him. If he should return, would there still be time? Lincoln was not at home. Where was he? Perhaps at a rendezvous with Madame Steno.

The image of that handsome idol of love clasped in the painter's arms, plunged in the abyss of intoxication which her ardent letters described, was presented to the mind of the jealous wife. What irony to perceive thus those two lovers, whom she had wished to strike, with the ecstacy of bliss in their eyes! Lydia would have liked to tear out their eyes, his as well as hers, and to trample them beneath her heel. A fresh flood of hatred filled her heart. God! how she hated them, and with what a powerless hatred! But her time would come; another need pressed sorely —to prevent the meeting of the following day, to save her brother. To whom should she turn, however? To Dorsenne? To Montfanon? To Baron Hafner? To Peppino Ardea? She thought by turns of the four personages whose almost simultaneous visits had caused her to believe that they were the seconds of the two champions. She rejected them, one after the other, comprehending that none of them possessed enough authority to arrange the affair. Her thoughts finally reverted to Florent's adversary, to Boleslas Gorka, whose wife was her friend and whom she had always found so courteous. What if she should ask him to spare her brother? It was not Florent against whom the discarded lover bore a grudge. Would he not be touched by her tears? Would he not tell her what had led to the quarrel and what she should ask of her brother that the quarrel might be conciliated? Could she not obtain from him the promise to discharge his weapon in the air, if the duel was with pistols, or, if it was with swords, simply to disarm his enemy?

Like nearly all persons unversed in the art, she believed in infallible fencers, in marksmen who never missed their aim, and she had also ideas profoundly, absolutely inexact on the relations of one man with another in the matter of an insult. But how can women admit that inflexible rigor in certain cases, which forms the foundation of manly relations, when they themselves allow of a similar rigor neither in their arguments with men, nor in their discussions among themselves? Accustomed always to appeal from convention to instinct and from reason to sentiment, they are, in the face of certain laws, be they those of justice or of honor, in a state of incomprehension worse than ignorance. A duel, for example, appears to them like an arbitrary drama, which the wish of one of those concerned can change at his fancy. Ninety-nine women out of a hundred would think like Lydia Maitland of hastening to the adversary of the man they love, to demand, to beg for his life. Let us add, however, that the majority would not carry out that thought. They would confine themselves to sewing in the vest of their beloved some blessed medal, in recommending him to the Providence, which, for them, is still the favoritism of heaven. Lydia felt that if ever Florent should learn of her step with regard to Gorka, he would be very indignant. But who would tell him? She was agitated by one of those fevers of fear and of remorse which are too acute not to act, cost what it might. Her carriage was announced, and she entered it, giving the address of the Palazzetto Doria. In what terms should she approach the man to whom she was about to pay that audacious and absurd visit? Ah, what mattered it? The circumstances would inspire her. Her desire to cut short the duel was so strong that she did not doubt of success.

She was greatly disappointed when the footman at the palace told her that the Count had gone out, while at the same moment a voice interrupted him with a gay laugh. It was Countess Maud Gorka, who, returning from her walk with her little boy, recognized Lydia's coup, and who said to her:

"What a lucky idea I had of returning a little sooner. I see you were afraid of a storm, as you drove out in a closed carriage. Will you come upstairs a moment?" And, perceiving that the young woman, whose hand she had taken, was trembling: "What ails you? I should think you were ill! You do not feel well? My God, what ails her! She is ill, Luc," she added, turning to her son; "run to my room and bring me the large bottle of English salts; Rose knows which one. Go, go quickly."

"It is nothing," replied Lydia, who had indeed closed her eyes as if on the point of swooning. "See, I am better already. I think I will return home; it will be wiser."

"I shall not leave you," said Maud, seating herself, too, in the carriage; and, as they handed her the bottle of salts, she made Madame Maitland inhale it, talking to her the while as to a sick child: "Poor little thing!"

"How her cheeks burn! And you pay visits in this state. It is very venturesome! Rue Leopardi," she called to the coachman, "quickly."

The carriage rolled away, and Madame Gorka continued to press the tiny hands of Lydia, to whom she gave the tender name, so ironical under the circumstances, of "Poor little one!" Maud was one of those women like whom England produces many, for the honor of that healthy and robust British civilization, who are at once all energy and all goodness. As large and stout as Lydia was slender, she would rather have borne her to her bed in her vigorous arms than to have abandoned her in the troubled state in which she had surprised her. Not less practical and, as her compatriots say, as matter-of-fact as she was charitable, she began to question her friend on the symptoms which had preceded that attack, when with astonishment she saw that altered face contract, tears gushing from the closed eyes, and the fragile form convulsed by sobs. Lydia had a nervous attack caused by anxiety, by the fresh disappointment of Boleslas's absence from home, and no doubt, too, by the gentleness with which Maud addressed her, and tearing her handkerchief with her white teeth, she moaned:

"No, I am not ill. But it is that thought which I can not bear. No, I can not. Ah, it is maddening!" And turning toward her companion, she in her turn pressed her hands, saying: "But you know nothing! You suspect nothing! It is that

14

which maddens me, when I see you tranquil, calm, happy, as if the minutes were not valuable, every one, to-day, to you as well as to me. For if one is my brother, the other is your husband; and you love him. You must love him, to have pardoned him for what you have pardoned him."

She had spoken in a sort of delirium, brought about by her extreme nervous excitement, and she had uttered, she, usually so dissembling, her very deepest thought. She did not think she was giving Madame Gorka any information by that allusion, so direct, to the liaison of Boleslas with Madame Steno. She was persuaded, as was entire Rome, that Maud knew of her husband's infidelities, and that she tolerated them by one of those heroic sacrifices which maternity justifies. How many women have immolated thus their wifely pride to maintain the domestic relation which the father shall at least not desert officially! All Rome was mistaken, and Lydia Maitland was to have an unexpected proof. Not a suspicion that such an intrigue could unite her husband with the mother of her best friend had ever entered the thoughts of Boleslas's wife. But to account for that, it is necessary to admit, as well, and to comprehend the depth of innocence of which, notwithstanding her twenty-six years, the beautiful and healthy Englishwoman, with her eyes so clear, so frank, was possessed.

She was one of those persons who command the respect of the boldest of men, and before whom the most dissolute women exercised care. She might have seen the freedom of Madame Steno without being disillusioned. She had only a liking for acquaintances and positive conversation. She was very intellectual, but without any desire to study character.

Dorsenne said of her, with more justness than he thought: "Madame Boleslas Gorka is married to a man who has never been presented to her," meaning by that, that first of all she had no idea of her husband's character, and then of the treason of which she was the victim. However, the novelist was not altogether right. Boleslas's infidelity was of too long standing for the woman passionately, religiously loyal, who was his wife, not to have suffered by it. But there was an abyss between such sufferings and the intuition of a determined fact such as that which Lydia had just mentioned, and such a suspicion was so far from Maud's thoughts that her companion's words only aroused in her astonishment at the mysterious danger of which Lydia's troubles was a proof more eloquent still than her words.

"Your brother? My husband?" she said. "I do not understand you."

"Naturally," replied Lydia, "he has hidden all from you, as Florent hid all from me. Well! They are going to fight a duel, and to-morrow morning…. Do not tremble, in your turn," she continued, twining her arms around Maud Gorka. "We shall be two to prevent the terrible affair, and we shall prevent it."

15

"A duel? To-morrow morning?" repeated Maud, in affright. "Boleslas fights to-morrow with your brother? No, it is impossible. Who told you so? How do you know it?"

"I read the proof of it with my eyes," replied Lydia. "I read Florent's will. I read the letter which he prepared for Maitland and for me in case of accident...."

"Should I be in the state in which you see me if it were not true?"

"Oh, I believe you!" cried Maud, pressing her hands to her eyelids, as if to shut out a horrible sight. "But where can they be seen? Boleslas has been here scarcely any of the time for two days. What is there between them? What have they said to one another? One does not risk one's life for nothing when he has, like Boleslas, a wife and a son. Answer me, I conjure you. Tell me all. I desire to know all. What is there at the bottom of this duel?"

"What could there be but a woman?" interrupted Lydia, who put into the two last words more savage scorn than if she had publicly spit in Caterina Steno's face. But that fresh access of anger fell before the surprise caused her by Madame Gorka's reply.

"What woman? I understand you still less than I did just now."

"When we are at home I will speak,".... replied Lydia, after having looked at Maud with a surprised glance, which was in itself the most terrible reply. The two women were silent. It was Maud who now required the sympathy of friendship, so greatly had the words uttered by Lydia startled her. The companion whose arm rested upon hers in that carriage, and who had inspired her with such pity fifteen minutes before, now rendered her fearful. She seemed to be seated by the side of another person. In the creature whose thin nostrils were dilated with passion, whose mouth was distorted with bitterness, whose eyes sparkled with anger, she no longer recognized little Madame Maitland, so taciturn, so reserved that she was looked upon as insignificant. What had that voice, usually so musical, told her; that voice so suddenly become harsh, and which had already revealed to her the great danger suspended over Boleslas? To what woman had that voice alluded, and what meant that sudden reticence?

Lydia was fully aware of the grief into which she would plunge Maud without the slightest premeditation. For a moment she thought it almost a crime to say more to a woman thus deluded. But at the same time she saw in the revelation two certain results. In undeceiving Madame Gorka she made a mortal enemy for Madame Steno, and, on the other hand, never would the woman so deeply in love with her husband allow him to fight for a former mistress. So, when they both entered the small salon of the Moorish mansion, Lydia's resolution was taken. She was determined to conceal nothing of what she knew from unhappy Maud, who asked her, with a beating heart, and in a voice choked by emotion:

"Now, will you explain to me what you want to say?"

"Question me," replied the other; "I will answer you. I have gone too far to draw back."

"You claimed that a woman was the cause of the duel between your brother and my husband?"

"I am sure of it," replied Lydia.

"What is that woman's name?"

"Madame Steno."

"Madame Steno?" repeated Maud. "Catherine Steno is the cause of that duel? How?"

"Because she is my husband's mistress," replied Lydia, brutally; "because she has been your husband's, because Gorka came here, mad with jealousy, to provoke Lincoln, and because he met my brother, who prevented him from entering…. They quarrelled, I know not in what manner. But I know the cause of the duel…. Am I right, yes or no, in telling you they are to fight about that woman?"

"My husband's mistress?" cried Maud. "You say Madame Steno has been my husband's mistress? It is not true. You lie! You lie! You lie! I do not believe it."

"You do not believe me?" said Lydia, shrugging her shoulders. "As if I had the least interest in deceiving you; as if one would lie when the life of the only being one loves in the world is in the balance! For I have only my brother, and perhaps to-morrow I shall no longer have him…. But you shall believe me. I desire that we both hate that woman, that we both be avenged upon her, as we both do not wish the duel to take place—the duel of which, I repeat, she is the cause, the sole cause…. You do not believe me? Do you know what caused your husband to return? You did not expect him; confess! It was I—I, do you hear— who wrote him what Steno and Lincoln were doing; day after day I wrote about their love, their meetings, their bliss. Ah, I was sure it would not be in vain, and he returned. Is that a proof?"

"You did not do that?" cried Madame Gorka, recoiling with horror. "It was infamous."

"Yes, I did it," replied Lydia, with savage pride, "and why not? It was my right when she took my husband from me. You have only to return and to look in the place where Gorka keeps his letters. You will certainly find those I wrote, and others, I assure you, from that woman. For she has a mania for letter-writing…. Do you believe me now, or will you repeat that I have lied?"

"Never," returned Maud, with sorrowful indignation upon her lovely, loyal face, "no, never will I descend to such baseness."

"Well, I will descend for you," said Lydia. "What you do not dare to do, I will dare, and you will ask me to aid you in being avenged. Come," and, seizing the hand of her stupefied companion, she drew her into Lincoln's studio, at that moment unoccupied. She approached one of those Spanish desks, called baygenos, and she touched two small panels, which disclosed, on opening, a secret drawer, in which were a package of letters, which she seized. Maud Gorka watched her with the same terrified horror with which she would have seen some one killed and robbed. That honorable soul revolted at the scene in which her mere presence made of her an accomplice. But at the same time she was a prey, as had been her husband several days before, to that maddening appetite to know the truth, which becomes, in certain forms of doubt, a physical need, as imperious as hunger and thirst, and she listened to Florent's sister, who continued:

"Will it be a proof when you have seen the affair written in her own hand? Yes," she continued, with cruel irony, "she loves correspondence, our fortunate rival. Justice must be rendered her that she may make no more avowals. She writes as she feels. It seems that the successor was jealous of his predecessor…. See, is this a proof this time?"…. And, after having glanced at the first letters as a person familiar with them, she handed one of those papers to Maud, who had not the courage to avert her eyes. What she saw written upon that sheet drew from her a cry of anguish. She had, however, only read ten lines, which proved how much mistaken psychological Dorsenne was in thinking that Maitland was ignorant of the former relations between his mistress and Gorka. Countess Steno's grandeur, that which made a courageous woman almost a heroine in her passions, was an absolute sincerity and disgust for the usual pettiness of flirtations. She would have disdained to deny to a new lover the knowledge of her past, and the semiavowals, so common to women, would have seemed to her a cowardice still worse. She had not essayed to hide from Maitland what connection she had broken off for him, and it was upon one of those phrases, in which she spoke of it openly, that Madame Gorka's eyes fell:

"You will be pleased with me," she wrote, "and I shall no longer see in your dear blue eyes which I kiss, as I love them, that gleam of mistrust which troubles me. I have stopped the correspondence with Gorka. If you require it, I will even break with Maud, notwithstanding the reason you know of and

18

which will render it difficult for me. But how can you be jealous yet?.... Is not my frankness with regard to that liaison the surest guarantee that it is ended? Come, do not be jealous. Listen to what I know so well, that I felt I loved, and that my life began only on the day when you took me in your arms. The woman you have awakened in me, no one has known—"

"She writes well, does she not?" said Lydia, with a gleam of savage triumph in her eyes. "Do you believe me, now?.... Do you see that we have the same interest to-day, a common affront to avenge? And we will avenge it.... Do you understand that you can not allow your husband to fight a duel with my brother? You owe that to me who have given you this weapon by which you hold him.... Threaten him with a divorce. Fortune is with you. The law will give you your child. I repeat, you hold him firmly. You will prevent the duel, will you not?"

"Ah! What do you think it matters to me now if they fight or not?" said Maud. "From the moment he deceived me was I not widowed? Do not approach me," she added, looking at Lydia with wild eyes, while a shudder of repulsion shook her entire frame.... "Do not speak to me.... I have as much horror of you as of him.... Let me go, let me leave here.... Even to feel myself in the same room with you fills me with horror.... Ah, what disgrace!"

She retreated to the door, fixing upon her informant a gaze which the other sustained, notwithstanding the scorn in it, with the gloomy pride of defiance. She went out repeating: "Ah, what disgrace!" without Lydia having addressed her, so greatly had surprise at the unexpected result of all her attempts paralyzed her. But the formidable creature lost no time in regret and repentance. She paused a few moments to think. Then, crushing in her nervous hand the letter she had shown Maud, at the risk of being discovered by her husband later, she said aloud:

"Coward! Lord, what a coward she is! She loves. She will pardon. Will there, then, be no one to aid me? No one to smite them in their insolent happiness." After meditating awhile, her face still more contracted, she placed the letter in the drawer, which she closed again, and half an hour later she summoned a commissionaire, to whom she intrusted a letter, with the order to deliver it immediately, and that letter was addressed to the inspector of police of the district. She informed him of the intended duel, giving him the names of the two adversaries and of the four seconds. If she had not been afraid of her brother, she would even that time have signed her name.

"I should have gone to work that way at first," said she to herself, when the door of the small salon closed behind the messenger to whom she had given her order personally. "The police know how to prevent them from fighting, even if I do not succeed with Florent.... As for him?".... and she looked at a portrait of Maitland upon the desk at which she had just been writing. "Were I to tell him what is taking place.... No, I will ask nothing of him.... I hate him too much.".... And she concluded with a fierce smile, which disclosed her teeth at the corners of her mouth:

"It is all the same. It is necessary that Maud Gorka work with me against her. There is some one whom she will not pardon, and that is.... Madame Steno." And, in spite of her uneasiness, the wicked woman trembled with delight at the thought of her work.

CHAPTER VIII

When Maud Gorka left the house on the Rue Leopardi she walked on at first rapidly, blindly, without seeing, without hearing anything, like a wounded animal which runs through the thicket to escape danger, to escape its wounds, to escape itself. It was a little more than half-past three o'clock when the unhappy woman hastened from the studio, unable to bear near her the presence of Lydia Maitland, of that sinister worker of vengeance who had so cruelly revealed to her, with such indisputable proofs, the atrocious affair, the long, the infamous, the inexpiable treason.

It was almost six o'clock before Maud Gorka really regained consciousness. A very common occurrence aroused her from the somnambulism of suffering in which she had wandered for two hours. The storm which had threatened since noon at length broke. Maud, who had scarcely heeded the first large drops, was forced to seek shelter when the clouds suddenly burst, and she took refuge at the right extremity of the colonnade of St. Peter's. How had she gone that far? She did not know herself precisely. She remembered vaguely that she had wandered through a labyrinth of small streets, had crossed the Tiber—no doubt by the Garibaldi bridge—had passed through a large garden —doubtless the Janicule, since she had walked along a portion of the ramparts. She had left the city by the Porte de Saint-Pancrace, to follow by that of Cavallegieri the sinuous line of the Urban walls.

That corner of Rome, with a view of the pines of the Villa Pamfili on one side, and on the other the back part of the Vatican, serves as a promenade during the winter for the few cardinals who go in search of the afternoon sun, certain there of meeting only a few strangers. In the month of May it is a desert, scorched by the sun, which glows upon the brick, discolored by two centuries of that implacable heat which caresses the scales of the green and gray lizards about to crawl between the bees of Pope Urbain VIII's escutcheon of the Barberini family. Madame Gorka's instinct had at least served her in leading her upon a route on which she met no one. Now the sense of reality returned. She recognized the objects around her, and that framework, so familiar to her piety of fervent Catholicism, the enormous square, the obelisk of Sixte-Quint in the centre, the fountains, the circular portico crowned with bishops and martyrs, the palace of the Vatican at the corner, and yonder the facade of the large papal cathedral, with the Saviour and the apostles erect upon the august pediment.

On any other occasion in life the pious young woman would have seen in the chance which led her thither, almost unconsciously, an influence from above, an invitation to enter the church, there to ask the strength to suffer of the God who said: "Let him who wishes follow me, let him renounce all, let him take up his cross and follow me!" But she was passing through that first bitter paroxysm of grief in which it is impossible to pray, so greatly does the revolt of nature cry out within us. Later, we may recognize the hand of Providence in the trial imposed upon us. We see at first only the terrible injustice of fate, and we tremble in the deepest recesses of our souls with rebellion at the blow from which we bleed. That which rendered the rebellion more invincible and more fierce in Maud, was the suddenness of the mortal blow.

Daily some pure, honest woman, like her, acquires the proof of the treason of a husband whom she has not ceased to love. Ordinarily, the indisputable proof is preceded by a long period of suspicion. The faithless one neglects his hearth. A change takes place in his daily habits. Various hints reveal to the outraged wife the trace of a rival, which woman's jealousy distinguishes with a scent as certain as that of a dog which finds a stranger in the house. And, finally, although there is in the transition from doubt to certainty a laceration of the heart, it is at least the laceration of a heart prepared. That preparation, that adaptation, so to speak, of her soul to the truth, Maud had been deprived of. The care taken by Madame Steno to strengthen the friendship between her and Alba had suppressed the slightest signs. Boleslas had no need to change his domestic life in order to see his mistress at his convenience and in an intimacy entertained, provoked, by his wife herself. The wife, too, had been totally, absolutely deceived. She had assisted in her husband's adultery with one of those illusions so complete that it seemed improbable to the indifferent and to strangers. The awakening from such illusions is the most terrible. That man whom society considered a complaisant husband, that woman who seemed so indulgent a wife, suddenly find that they have committed a murder or a suicide, to the great astonishment of the world which, even then, hesitates to recognize in that access of folly the proof, the blow, more formidable, more instantaneous in its ravages, than those of love-sudden disillusion. When the disaster is not interrupted by acts of violence, it causes an irreparable destruction of the youthfulness of the soul, it is the idea instilled in us forever that all can betray, since we have been betrayed in that manner. It is for years, for life, sometimes, that powerlessness to be affected, to hope, to believe, which caused Maud Gorka to remain, on that afternoon, leaning against the pedestal of a column, watching the rain fall, instead of ascending to the Basilica, where the confessional offers pardon for all sins and the remedy for all sorrows. Alas! It was consolation simply to kneel there, and the poor woman was only in the first stage of Calvary.

She watched the rain fall, and she found a savage comfort in the formidable character of the storm, which seemed like a cataclysm of nature, to such degree did the flash of the lightning and the roar of the thunder mingle with the echoes of the vast palace beneath the lash of the wind. Forms began to take shape in her mind, after the whirlwind of blind suffering in which she felt herself borne away after the first glance cast upon that fatal letter. Each word rose before her eyes, so feverish that she closed them with pain. The last two years of her life, those which had bound her to Countess Steno, returned to her thoughts, illuminated by a brilliance which drew from her constantly these words, uttered with a moan: How could he? She saw Venice and their sojourn in the villa to which Boleslas had conducted her after the death of their little girl, in order that there, in the restful atmosphere of the lagoon, she might overcome the keen paroxysm of pain.

How very kind and delicate Madame Steno had been at that time; at least how kind she had seemed, and how delicate likewise, comprehending her grief and sympathizing with it…. Their superficial relations had gradually ripened into friendship. Then, no doubt, the treason had begun. The purloiner of love had introduced herself under cover of the pity in which Maud had believed. Seeing the Countess so generous, she had treated as calumny the slander of the world relative to a person capable of such touching kindness of heart. And it was at that moment that the false woman took Boleslas from her! A thousand details recurred to her which at the time she had not understood; the sails of the two lovers in the gondola, which she had not even thought of suspecting; a visit which Boleslas had made to Piove and from which he only returned the following day, giving as a pretext a missed train; words uttered aside on the balcony of the Palais Steno at night, while she talked with Alba. Yes, it was at Venice that their adultery began, before her who had divined nothing, her whose heart was filled with inconsolable regret for her lost darling! Ah, how could he? she moaned again, and the visions multiplied.

In her mind were then opened all the windows which Gorka's perfidity and the Countess's as well, had sealed with such care. She saw again the months which followed their return to Rome, and that mode of life so convenient for both. How often had she walked out with Alba, thus freeing the mother and the husband from the only surveillance annoying to them. What did the lovers do during those hours? How many times on returning to the Palazzetto Doria had she found Catherine Steno in the library, seated on the divan beside Boleslas, and she had not mistrusted that the woman had come, during her absence, to embrace that man, to talk to him of love, to give herself to him, without doubt, with the charm of villainy and of danger! She remembered the episode of their meeting at Bayreuth the previous summer, when she went to England alone with her son, and when her husband undertook to conduct Alba and the Countess from Rome to Bavaria. They had all met at Nuremberg. The apartments of the hotel in which the meeting took place became again very vivid in Maud's memory, with Madame Steno's bedroom adjoining that of Boleslas's.

The vision of their caresses, enjoyed in the liberty of the night, while innocent Alba slept near by, and when she rolled away in a carriage with little Luc, drew from her this cry once more: "Ah, how could he!".... And immediately that vision awoke in her the remembrance of her husband's recent return. She saw him traversing Europe on the receipt of an anonymous letter, to reach that woman's side twenty-four hours sooner. What a proof of passion was the frenzy which had not allowed him any longer to bear doubt and absence!.... Did he love the mistress who did not even love him, since she had deceived him with Maitland? And he was going to fight a duel on her account!.... Jealousy, at that moment, wrung the wife's heart with a pang still stronger than that of indignation. She, the strong Englishwoman, so large, so robust, almost masculine in form, mentally compared herself with the supple Italian with her form so round, with her gestures so graceful, her hands so delicate, her feet so dainty; compared herself with the creature of desire, whose every movement implied a secret wave of passion, and she ceased her cry— "Ah, how could he?"—at once. She had a clear knowledge of the power of her rival.

It is indeed a supreme agony for an honorable woman, who loves, to feel herself thus degraded by the mere thought of the intoxication her husband has tasted in arms more beautiful, more caressing, more entwining than hers. It was, too, a signal for the return of will to the tortured but proud soul. Disgust possessed her, so violent, so complete, for the atmosphere of falsehood and of sensuality in which Boleslas had lived two years, that she drew herself up, becoming again strong and implacable. Braving the storm, she turned in the direction of her home, with this resolution as firmly rooted in her mind as if she had deliberated for months and months.

"I will not remain with that man another day. Tomorrow I will leave for England with my son."

How many, in a similar situation, have uttered such vows, to abjure them when they find themselves face to face with the man who has betrayed them, and whom they love. Maud was not of that order. Certainly she loved dearly the seductive Boleslas, wedded against her parents' will the perfidious one for whom she had sacrificed all, living far from her native land and her family for years, because it pleased him, breathing, living, only for him and for their boy. But there was within her—as her long, square chin, her short nose and the strength of her brow revealed— the force of inflexibility—which is met

24

with in characters of an absolute uprightness. Love, with her, could be stifled by disgust, or, rather, she considered it degrading to continue to love one whom she scorned, and, at that moment, it was supreme scorn which reigned in her heart. She had, in the highest degree, the great virtue which is found wherever there is nobility, and of which the English have made the basis of their moral education—the religion, the fanaticism of loyalty. She had always grieved on discovering the wavering nature of Boleslas. But if she had observed in him, with sorrow, any exaggerations of language, any artificial sentiment, a dangerous suppleness of mind, she had pardoned him those defects with the magnanimity of love, attributing them to a defective training. Gorka at a very early age had witnessed a stirring family drama—his mother and his father lived apart, while neither the one nor the other had the exclusive guidance of the child. How could she find indulgence for the shameful hypocrisy of two years' standing, for the villainy of that treachery practised at the domestic hearth, for the continued, voluntary disloyalty of every day, every hour? Though Maud experienced, in the midst of her despair, the sort of calmness which proves a firm and just resolution, when she reentered the Palazzetto Doria—what a drama had been enacted in her heart since her going out!—and it was in a voice almost as calm as usual that she asked: "Is the Count at home?"

What did she experience when the servant, after answering her in the affirmative, added: "Madame and Mademoiselle Steno, too, are awaiting Madame in the salon." At the thought that the woman who had stolen from her her husband was there, the betrayed wife felt her blood boil, to use a common but expressive phrase. It was very natural that Alba's mother should call upon her, as was her custom. It was still more natural for her to come there that day. For very probably a report of the duel the following day had reached her. Her presence, however, and at that moment, aroused in Maud a feeling of indignation so impassioned that her first impulse was to enter, to drive out Boleslas's mistress as one would drive out a servant surprised thieving. Suddenly the thought of Alba presented itself to her mind, of that sweet and pure Alba, of that soul as pure as her name, of her whose dearest friend she was. Since the dread revelation she had thought several times of the young girl. But her deep sorrow having absorbed all the power of her soul, she had not been able to feel such friendship for the delicate and pretty child. At the thought of ejecting her rival, as she had the right to do, that sentiment stirred within her. A strange pity flooded her soul, which caused her to pause in the centre of the large hall, ornamented with statues and columns, which she was in the act of crossing. She called the servant just as he was about to put his hand on the knob of the door. The analogy between her situation and that of Alba struck her very forcibly. She experienced the sensation which

Alba had so often experienced in connection with Fanny, sympathy with a sorrow so like her own. She could not give her hand to Madame Steno after what she had discovered, nor could she speak to her otherwise than to order her from her house. And to utter before Alba one single phrase, to make one single gesture which would arouse her suspicions, would be too implacable, too iniquitous a vengeance! She turned toward the door which led to her own room, bidding the servant ask his master to come thither. She had devised a means of satisfying her just indignation without wounding her dear friend, who was not responsible for the fact that the two culprits had taken shelter behind her innocence.

Having entered the small, pretty boudoir which led into her bedroom, she seated herself at her desk, on which was a photograph of Madame Steno, in a group consisting of Boleslas, Alba, and herself. The photograph smiled with a smile of superb insolence, which suddenly reawakened in the outraged woman her frenzy of rancor, interrupted or rather suspended for several moments by pity. She took the frame in her hands, she cast it upon the ground, trampling the glass beneath her feet, then she began to write, on the first blank sheet, one of those notes which passion alone dares to pen, which does not draw back at every word:

"I know all. For two years you have been my husband's mistress. Do not deny it. I have read the confession written by your own hand. I do not wish to see nor to speak to you again. Never again set foot in my house. On account of your daughter I have not driven you out to-day. A second time I shall not hesitate."

She was just about to sign Maud Gorka, when the sound of the door opening and shutting caused her to turn. Boleslas was before her. Upon his face was an ambiguous expression, which exasperated the unhappy wife still more. Having returned more than an hour before, he had learned that Maud had accompanied to the Rue Leopardi Madame Maitland, who was ill, and he awaited her return with impatience, agitated by the thought that Florent's sister was no doubt ill owing to the duel of the morrow, and in that case, Maud, too, would know all. There are conversations and, above all, adieux which a man who is about to fight a duel always likes to avoid. Although he forced a smile, he no longer doubted. His wife's evident agitation could not be explained by any other cause. Could he divine that she had learned not only of the duel, but, too, of an intrigue that day ended and of which she had known nothing for two years? As she was silent, and as that silence embarrassed him, he tried, in order to keep him in countenance, to take her hand and kiss it, as was his custom. She repelled him with a look which he had never seen upon her face and said to him, handing him the sheet of paper lying before her:

"Do you wish to read this note before I send it to Madame Steno, who is in the salon with her daughter?"

Boleslas took the letter. He read the terrible lines, and he became livid. His agitation was so great that he returned the paper to his wife without replying, without attempting to prevent, as was his duty, the insult offered to his former mistress, whom he still loved to the point of risking his life for her. That man, so brave and so yielding at once, was overwhelmed by one of those surprises which put to flight all the powers of the mind, and he watched Maud slip the note into an envelope, write the address and ring. He heard her say to the servant:

"You will take this note to Countess Steno and you will excuse me to the ladies…. I feel too indisposed to receive any one. If they insist, you will reply that I have forbidden you to admit any one. You understand—any one."

The man took the note. He left the room and he had no doubt fulfilled his errand while the husband and wife stood there, face to face, neither of them breaking the formidable silence. They felt that the hour was a solemn one.

Never, since the day on which Cardinal Manning had united their destinies in the chapel of Ardrahan Castle, had they been engaged in a crisis so tragical. Such moments lay bare the very depths of the character. Courageous and noble, Maud did not think of weighing her words. She did not try to feed her jealousy, nor to accentuate the cruelty of the cause of the insult which she had the right to launch at the man toward whom that very morning she had been so confiding, so tender. The baseness and the cruelty were to remain forever unknown to the woman who no longer hesitated as to the bold resolution she had made. No. That which she expected of the man whom she had loved so dearly, of whom she had entertained so exalted an opinion, whom she had just seen fall so low, was a cry of truth, an avowal in which she would find the throb of a last remnant of honor. If he were silent it was not because he was preparing a denial. The tenor of Maud's letter left no doubt as to the nature of the proofs she had in her hand, which she had there no doubt. How? He did not ask himself that question, governed as he was by a phenomenon in which was revealed to the full the singular complexity of his nature. The Slav's especial characteristic is a prodigious, instantaneous nervousness. It seems that those beings with the uncertain hearts have a faculty of amplifying in themselves, to the point of absorbing the heart altogether, states of partial, passing, and yet sincere emotion. The intensity of their momentary excitement thus makes of them sincere comedians, who speak to you as if they felt certain sentiments of an exclusive order, to feel contradictory ones the day after, with the same ardor, with the same untruthfulness, unjustly say the victims of those natures, so much the more deceitful as they are more vibrating.

He suffered, indeed, on discovering that Maud had been initiated into his criminal intrigue, but he suffered more for her than for himself. It was sufficient for that suffering to occupy a few moments, a few hours. It reinvested the personality of the impassioned and weak husband who loved his wife while betraying her. There was, indeed, a shade of it in his adventure, but a very slight shade. And yet, he did not think he was telling an untruth, when he finally broke the silence to say to her whom he had so long deceived:

"You have avenged yourself with much severity, Maud, but you had the right.... I do not know who has informed you of an error which was very culpable, very wrong, very unfortunate, too.... I know that I have in Rome enemies bent upon my ruin, and I am sure they have left me no means of defending myself. I have deceived you, and I have suffered."

He paused after those words, uttered with a tremor of conviction which was not assumed. He had forgotten that ten minutes before he had entered the room with the firm determination to hide his duel and its cause from the woman for whose pardon he would at that moment have sacrificed his life without hesitation. He continued, in a voice softened by affection: "Whatever they have told you, whatever you have read, I swear to you, you do not know all."

"I know enough," interrupted Maud, "since I know that you have been the lover of that woman, of the mother of my intimate friend, at my side, under my very eyes.... If you had suffered by that deception, as you say, you would not have waited to avow all to me until I held in my hands the undeniable proof of your infamy.... You have cast aside the mask, or, rather, I have wrested it from you.... I desire no more.... As for the details of the shameful story, spare me them. It was not to hear them that I reentered a house every corner of which reminds me that I believed in you implicitly, and that you have betrayed me, not one day, but every day; that you betrayed me the day before yesterday, yesterday, this morning, an hour ago.... I repeat, that is sufficient."

"But it is not sufficient for me!" exclaimed Boleslas. "Yes, all you have just said is true, and I deserve to have you tell it to me. But that which you could not read in those letters shown to you, that which I have kept for two years in the depths of my heart, and which must now be told—is that, through all these fatal impulses, I have never ceased to love you.... Ah, do not recoil from me, do not look at me thus.... I feel it once more in the agony I have suffered since you are speaking to me; there is something within me that has never ceased being yours. That woman has been my aberration. She has had my madness, my senses, my passion, all the evil instincts of my being.... You have remained my idol, my affection, my religion…. If I lied to you it was because I knew that the day on which you would find out my fault I should see you before me, despairing and implacable as you now are, as I can not bear to have you be. Ah, judge me, condemn me, curse me; but know, but feel, that in spite of all I have loved you, I still love you."

Again he spoke with an enthusiasm which was not feigned. Though he had deceived her, he recognized only too well the value of the loyal creature before him, whom he feared he should lose. If he could not move her at the moment when he was about to fight a duel, when could he move her? So he approached her with the same gesture of suppliant and impassioned adoration which he employed in the early days of their marriage, and before his treason, when he had told her of his love. No doubt that remembrance thrust itself upon Maud and disgusted her, for it was with veritable horror that she again recoiled, replying:

"Be silent! That lie is the worst of all. It pains me. I blush for you, in seeing that you have not even the courage to acknowledge your fault. God is my witness, I should have respected you more, had you said: 'I have ceased loving you. I have taken a mistress. It was convenient for me to lie to you. I have lied. I have sacrificed all to my passion, my honor, my duties, my vows and you.'…. Ah, speak to me like that, that I may have with you the sentiment of truth…. But that you dare to repeat to me words of tenderness after what you have done to me, inspires me with repulsion. It is too bitter."

"Yes," said Boleslas, "you think thus. True and simple as you are, how could you have learned to understand what a weak will is—a will which wishes and which does not, which rises and which falls?…. And yet, if I had not loved you, what interest would I have in lying to you? Have I anything to conceal now? Ah, if you knew in what a position I am, on the eve of what day, I beseech you to believe that at least the best part of my being has never ceased to be yours!"

It was the strongest effort he could make to bring back the heart of his wife so deeply wounded—the allusion to his duel. For since she had not mentioned it to him, it was no doubt because she was still ignorant of it. He was once more startled by the reply she made, and which proved to him to what a degree indignation had paralyzed even her love. He resumed:

"Do you know it?"

"I know that you fight a duel to-morrow," said she, "and for your mistress, I know, too."

"It is not true," he exclaimed; "it is not for her."

"What?" asked Maud, energetically. "Was it not on her account that you went to the Rue Leopardi to provoke your rival? For she is not even true to you, and it is justice. Was it not on her account that you wished to enter the house, in spite of that rival's brother-in-law, and that a dispute arose between you, followed by this challenge? Was it not on her account, and to revenge yourself, that you returned from Poland, because you had received anonymous letters which told you all? And to know all has not disgusted you forever with that creature?.... But if she had deigned to lie to you, she would have you still at her feet, and you dare to tell me that you love me when you have not even cared to spare me the affront of learning all that villainy—all that baseness, all that disgrace—through some one else?"

"Who was it?" he asked. "Name that Judas to me, at least?"

"Do not speak thus," interrupted Maud, bitterly; "you have lost the right.... And then do not seek too far.... I have seen Madame Maitland to-day."

"Madame Maitland?" repeated Boleslas. "Did Madame Maitland denounce me to you? Did Madame Maitland write those anonymous letters?"

"She desired to be avenged," replied Maud, adding: "She has the right, since your mistress robbed her of her husband."

"Well, I, too, will be avenged!" exclaimed the young man. "I will kill that husband for her, after I have killed her brother. I will kill them both, one after the other."…. His mobile countenance, which had just expressed the most impassioned of supplications, now expressed only hatred and rage, and the same change took place in his immoderate sensibility. "Of what use is it to try to settle matters?" he continued. "I see only too well all is ended between us. Your pride and your rancor are stronger than your love. If it had been otherwise, you would have begged me not to fight, and you would only have reproached me, as you have the right to do, I do not deny.... But from the moment that you no longer love me, woe to him whom I find in my path! Woe to Madame Maitland and to those she loves!"

"This time at least you are sincere," replied Maud, with renewed bitterness. "Do you think I have not suffered sufficient humiliation? Would you like me to supplicate you not to fight for that creature? And do you not feel the supreme outrage which that encounter is to me? Moreover," she continued with tragical solemnity, "I did not summon you to have with you a conversation as sad as it is useless, but to tell you my resolution.... I hope that you will not oblige me to resort for its execution to the means which the law puts in my power?"

"I don't deserve to be spoken to thus," said Boleslas, haughtily.

"I will remain here to-night," resumed Maud, without heeding that reply, "for the last time. To-morrow evening I shall leave for England."

"You are free," said he, with a bow.

"And I shall take my son with me," she added.

"Our son!" he replied, with the composure of a man overcome by an access of tenderness and who controls himself. "That? No. I forbid it."

"You forbid it?" said she. "Very well, we will appeal it. I knew that you would force me," she continued, haughtily, in her turn, "to have recourse to the law…. But I shall not recoil before anything. In betraying me as you have done, you have also betrayed our child. I will not leave him to you. You are not worthy of him."

"Listen, Maud," said Boleslas, sadly, after a pause, "remember that it is perhaps the last time we shall meet…. To-morrow, if I am killed, you shall do as you like…. If I live, I promise to consent to any arrangement that will be just…. What I ask of you is—and I have the right, notwithstanding my faults —in the name of our early years of wedded life, in the name of that son himself, to leave me in a different way, to have a feeling, I don't say of pardon, but of pity."

"Did you have it for me," she replied, "when you were following your passion by way of my heart? No!".… And she walked before him in order to reach the door, fixing upon him eyes so haughty that he involuntarily lowered his. "You have no longer a wife and I have no longer a husband…. I am no Madame Maitland; I do not avenge myself by means of anonymous letters nor by denunciation…. But to pardon you?…. Never, do you hear, never!"

With those words she left the room, with those words into which she put all the indomitable energy of her character…. Boleslas did not essay to detain her. When, an hour after that horrible conversation, his valet came to inform him that dinner was served, the wretched man was still in the same place, his elbow on the mantelpiece and his forehead in his hand. He knew Maud too well to hope that she would change her determination, and there was in him, in spite of his faults, his folly and his complications, too much of the real gentleman to employ means of violence and to detain her forcibly, when he had erred so gravely. So she went thus. If, just before, he had exaggerated the expression of his feelings in saying, in thinking rather, that he had never ceased loving her, it was true that amid all his errors he had maintained for her an affection composed particularly of gratitude, remorse, esteem and, it must be said, of selfishness.

He loved for the devotion of which he was absolutely sure, and then, like many husbands who deceive an irreproachable wife, he was proud of her, while unfaithful to her. She seemed to him at once the dignity and the charity of his life. She had remained in his eyes the one to whom he could always return, the assured friend of moments of trial, the haven after the tempest, the moral peace when he was weary of the troubles of passion. What life would he lead when she was gone? For she would go! Her resolution was irrevocable. All dropped from his side at once. The mistress, to whom he had sacrificed the noblest and most loving heart, he had lost under circumstances as abject as their two years of passion had been dishonorable. His wife was about to leave him, and would he succeed in keeping his son? He had returned to be avenged, and he had not even succeeded in meeting his rival. That being so impressionable had experienced, in the face of so many repeated blows, a disappointment so absolute that he gladly looked forward to the prospect of exposing himself to death on the following day, while at the same time a bitter flood of rancor possessed him at the thought of all the persons concerned in his adventure. He would have liked to crush Madame Steno and Maitland, Lydia and Florent—Dorsenne, too—for having given him the false word of honor, which had strengthened still more his thirst for vengeance by calming it for a few hours.

His confusion of thoughts was only greater when he was seated alone with his son at dinner. That morning he had seen before him his wife's smiling face. The absence of her whom at that moment he valued above all else was so sad to him that he ventured one last attempt, and after the meal he sent little Luc to see if his mother would receive him. The child returned with a reply in the negative. "Mamma is resting.... She does not wish to be disturbed." So the matter was irremissible. She would not see her husband until the morrow—if he lived. For vainly did Boleslas convince himself that afternoon that he had lost none of his skill in practising before his admiring seconds; a duel is always a lottery. He might be killed, and if the possibility of an eternal separation had not moved the injured woman, what prayer would move her? He saw her in his thoughts—her who at that moment, with blinds drawn, all lights subdued, endured in the semi-darkness that suffering which curses but does not pardon. Ah, but that sight was painful to him! And, in order that she might at least know how he felt, he took their son in his arms, and, pressing him to his breast, said: "If you see your mother before I do, you will tell her that we spent a very lonesome evening without her, will you not?"

"Why, what ails you?" exclaimed the child. "You have wet my cheeks with tears—you are sweeping!"

"You will tell her that, too, promise me," replied the father, "so that she will take good care of herself, seeing how we love her."

"But," said the little boy, "she was not ill when we walked together after breakfast. She was so gay."

"I think, too, it will be nothing serious," replied Gorka. He was obliged to dismiss his son and to go out. He felt so horribly sad that he was physically afraid to remain alone in the house. But whither should he go? Mechanically he repaired to the club, although it was too early to meet many of the members there. He came upon Pietrapertosa and Cibo, who had dined there, and who, seated on one of the divans, were conferring in whispers with the gravity of two ambassadors discussing the Bulgarian or Egyptian question.

"You have a very nervous air," they said to Boleslas, "you who were in such good form this afternoon."

"Yes," said Cibo, "you should have dined with us as we asked you to."

"When one is to fight a duel," continued Pietrapertosa, sententiously, "one should see neither one's wife nor one's mistress. Madame Gorka suspects nothing, I hope?"

"Absolutely nothing," replied Boleslas; "you are right. I should have done better not to have left you. But, here I am. We will exorcise dismal thoughts by playing cards and supping!"

"By playing cards and supping!" exclaimed Pietrapertosa. "And your hand? Think of your hand…. You will tremble, and you will miss your man."

"Alright dinner," said Cibo, "to bed at ten o'clock, up at six-thirty, and two eggs with a glass of old port is the recipe Machault gives."

"And which I shall not follow," said Boleslas, adding: "I give you my word that if I had no other cause for care than this duel, you would not see me in this condition." He uttered that phrase in a tragical voice, the sincerity of which the two Italians felt. They looked at each other without speaking. They were too shrewd and too well aware of the simplest scandals of Rome not to have divined the veritable cause of the encounter between Florent and Boleslas. On the other hand, they knew the latter too well not to mistrust somewhat his attitudes. However, there was such simple emotion in his accent that they spontaneously pitied him, and, without another word, they no longer opposed the caprices of their strange client, whom they did not leave until two o'clock in the morning —and fortune favored them. For they found themselves at the end of a game, recklessly played, each the richer by two or three hundred louis apiece. That meant a few days more in Paris on the next visit. They, too, truly regretted their friend's luck, saying, on separating:

"I very much fear for him," said Cibo. "Such luck at gaming, the night before a duel—bad sign, very bad sign."

"So much the more so that some one was there," replied Pietrapertosa, making with his fingers the sign which conjures the jettutura. For nothing in the world would he have named the personages against whose evil eye he provided in that manner. But Cibo understood him, and, drawing from his trousers pocket his watch, which he fastened a l'anglaise by a safety chain to his belt, he pointed out among the charms a golden horn:

"I have not let it go this evening," said he. "The worst is, that Gorka will not sleep, and then, his hand!"

Only the first of those two prognostics was to be verified. Returning home at that late hour, Boleslas did not even retire. He employed the remainder of the night in writing a long letter to his wife, one to his son, to be given to him on his eighteenth birthday, all in case of an accident. Then he examined his papers and he came upon the package of letters he had received from Madame Steno. Merely to reread a few of them, and to glance at the portraits of that faithless mistress again, heightened his anger to such a degree that he enclosed the whole in a large envelope, which he addressed to Lincoln Maitland. He had no sooner sealed it than he shrugged his shoulders, saying: "Of what use?" He raised the piece of material which stopped up the chimney, and, placing the envelope on the fire-dogs, he set it on fire. He shook with the tongs the remains of that which had been the most ardent, the most complete passion of his life, and he relighted the flames under the pieces of paper still intact. The unreasonable employment of a night which might be his last had scarcely paled his face. But his friends, who knew him well, started on seeing him with that impassively sinister countenance when he alighted from his phaeton, at about eight o'clock, at the inn selected for the meeting. He had ordered the carriage the day before to allay his wife's suspicions by the pretense of taking one of his usual morning drives. In his mental confusion he had forgotten to give a counter order, and that accident caused him to escape the two policemen charged by the questorship to watch the Palazzetto Doria, on Lydia Maitland's denunciation. The hired victoria, which those agents took, soon lost track of the swift English horses, driven as a man of his character and of his mental condition could drive.

The precaution of Chapron's sister was, therefore, baffled in that direction, and she succeeded no better with regard to her brother, who, to avoid all explanation with Lincoln, had gone, under the pretext of a visit to the country, to dine and sleep at the hotel. It was there that Montfanon and Dorsenne met him to conduct him to the rendezvous in the classical landau. Hardly had they reached the eminence of the circus of Maxence, on the Appian Way, when they were passed by Boleslas's phaeton.

"You can rest very easy," said Montfanon to Florent. "How can one aim correctly when one tires one's arm in that way?"

That had been the only allusion to the duel made between the three men during the journey, which had taken about an hour. Florent talked as he usually did, asking all sorts of questions which attested his care for minute information—the most of which might be utilized by his brother- in-law-and the Marquis had replied by evoking, with his habitual erudition, several of the souvenirs which peopled that vast country, strewn with tombs, aqueducts, ruined villas, with the line of the Monts Albains enclosing them beyond.

Dorsenne was silent. It was the first affair at which he had assisted, and his nervous anxiety was extreme.

Tragical presentiments oppressed him, and at the same time he apprehended momentarily that, Montfanon's religious scruples reawakening, he would not only have to seek another second, but would have to defer a solution so near. However, the struggle which was taking place in the heart of the "old leaguer" between the gentleman and the Christian, was displayed during the drive only by an almost imperceptible gesture. As the carriage passed the entrance to the catacomb of St. Calixtus, the former soldier of the Pope turned away his head. Then he resumed the conversation with redoubled energy, to pause in his turn, however, when the landau took, a little beyond the Tomb of Caecilia, a transverse road in the direction of the Ardeatine Way. It was there that 'l'Osteria del tempo perso' was built, upon the ground belonging to Cibo, on which the duel was to take place.

Before l'Osteria, whose signboard was surmounted by the arms of Pope Innocent VIII, three carriages were already waiting—Gorka's phaeton, a landau which had brought Cibo, Pietrapertosa and the doctor, and a simple botte, in which a porter had come. That unusual number of vehicles seemed likely to attract the attention of riflemen out for a stroll, but Cibo answered for the discretion of the innkeeper, who indeed cherished for his master the devotion of vassal to lord, still common in Italy. The three newcomers had no need to make the slightest explanation. Hardly had they alighted from the carriage, when the maid conducted them through the hall, where at that moment two huntsmen were breakfasting, their guns between their knees, and who, like true Romans, scarcely deigned to glance at the strangers, who passed from the common hall into a small court, from that court, through a shed, into a large field enclosed by boards, with here and there a few pine-trees.

That rather odd duelling-ground had formerly served Cibo as a paddock. He had essayed to increase his slender income by buying at a bargain some jaded horses, which he intended fattening by means of rest and good fodder, and then selling to cabmen, averaging a small profit. The speculation having miscarried, the place was neglected and unused, save under circumstances similar to those of this particular morning.

"We have arrived last," said Montfanon, looking at his watch; "we are, however, five minutes ahead of time. Remember," he added in a low voice, turning to Florent, "to keep the body well in the background," these words being followed by other directions.

"Thanks," replied Florent, who looked at the Marquis and Dorsenne with a glance which he ordinarily had only for Lincoln, "and you know that, whatever may come, I thank you for all from the depths of my heart."

The young man put so much grace in that adieu, his courage was so simple, his sacrifice for his brother-in-law so magnanimous and natural—in fact, for two days both seconds had so fully appreciated the charm of that disposition, absolutely free from thoughts of self—that they pressed his hand with the emotion of true friends. They were themselves, moreover, interested, and at once began the series of preparations without which the role of assistant would be physically insupportable to persons endowed with a little sensibility. In experienced hands like those of Montfanon, Cibo and Pietrapertosa, such preliminaries are speedily arranged. The code is as exact as the step of a ballet. Twenty minutes after the entrance of the last arrivals, the two adversaries were face to face. The signal was given. The two shots were fired simultaneously, and Florent sank upon the grass which covered the enclosure. He had a bullet in his thigh.

Dorsenne has often related since, as a singular trait of literary mania, that at the moment the wounded man fell he, himself, notwithstanding the anxiety which possessed him, had watched Montfanon, to study him. He adds that never had he seen a face express such sorrowful piety as that of the man who, scorning all human respect, made the sign of the cross. It was the devotee of the catacombs, who had left the altar of the martyrs to accomplish a work of charity, then carried away by anger so far as to place himself under the necessity of participating in a duel, who was, no doubt, asking pardon of God. What remorse was stirring within the heart of the fervent, almost mystical Christian, so strangely mixed up in an adventure of that kind? He had at least this comfort, that after the first examination, and when they had borne Florent into a room prepared hastily by the care of Cibo, the doctor declared himself satisfied. The ball could even be removed at once, and as neither the bone nor the muscles had been injured it was a matter of a few weeks at the most.

"All that now remains for us," concluded Cibo, who had brought back the news, "is to draw up our official report."

At that instant, and as the witnesses were preparing to reenter the house for the last formality, an incident occurred, very unexpected, which was to transform the encounter, up to that time so simple, into one of those memorable duels which are talked over at clubs and in armories. If Pietrapertosa and Cibo had ceased since morning to believe in the jettatura of the "some one" whom neither had named, it must be acknowledged that they were very unjust, for the good fortune of having gained something wherewith to swell their Parisian purses was surely naught by the side of this—to have to discuss with the Cavals, the Machaults and other professionals the case, almost unprecedented, in which they were participants.

Boleslas Gorka, who, when once his adversary had fallen, paced to and fro without seeming to care as to the gravity of the wound, suddenly approached the group formed by the four men, and in a tone of voice which did not predict the terrible aggression in which he was about to indulge, he said:

"One moment, gentlemen. I desire to say a few words in your presence to Monsieur Dorsenne."

"I am at your service, Gorka," replied Julien, who did not suspect the hostile intention of his old friend. He did not divine the form which that hostility was about to take, but he had always upon his mind his word of honor falsely given, and he was prepared to answer for it.

"It will not take much time, sir," continued Boleslas, still with the same insolently formal politeness, "you know we have an account to settle…. But as I have some cause not to believe in the validity of your honor, I should like to remove all cause of evasion." And before any one could interfere in the unheard-of proceedings he had raised his glove and struck Dorsenne in the face. As Gorka spoke, the writer turned pale. He had not the time to reply to the audacious insult offered him by a similar one, for the three witnesses of the scene cast themselves between him and his aggressor. He, however, pushed them aside with a resolute air.

"Remember, sirs," said he, "that by preventing me from inflicting on Monsieur Gorka the punishment he deserves, you force me to obtain another reparation. And I demand it immediately…. I will not leave this place," he continued, "without having obtained it."

"Nor I, without having given it to you," replied Boleslas. "It is all I ask."

"No, Dorsenne," cried Montfanon, who had been the first to seize the raised arm of the writer, "you shall not fight thus. First, you have no right. It requires at least twenty-four hours between the provocation and the encounter…. And you, sirs, must not agree to serve as seconds for Monsieur Gorka, after he has failed in a manner so grave in all the rules of the ground…. If you lend yourselves to it, it is barbarous, it is madness, whatsoever you like. It is no longer a duel."

"I repeat, Montfanon," replied Dorsenne, "that I will not leave here and that I will not allow Monsieur Gorka to leave until I have obtained the reparation to which I feel I have the right."

"And I repeat that I am at Monsieur Dorsenne's service," replied Boleslas.

"Very well, sirs," said Montfanon. "There only remains for us to leave you to arrange it one with the other as you wish, and for us to withdraw…. Is not that your opinion?" he continued, addressing Cibo and Pietrapertosa, who did not reply immediately.

"Certainly," finally said one; "the case is difficult."

"There are, however, precedents," insinuated the other.

"Yes," resumed Cibo, "if it were only the two successive duels of Henry de Pene."

"Which furnish authority," concluded Pietrapertosa.

"Authority has nothing to do with it," again exclaimed Montfanon. "I know, for my part, that I am not here to assist at a butchery, and that I will not assist at it…. I am going, sirs, and I expect you will do the same, for I do not suppose you would select coachmen to play the part of seconds…. Adieu, Dorsenne…. You do not doubt my friendship for you…. I think I am giving you a veritable proof of it by not permitting you to fight under such conditions."

When the old nobleman reentered the inn, he waited ten minutes, persuaded that his departure would determine that of Cibo and of Pietrapertosa, and that the new affair, following so strangely upon the other, would be deferred until the next day. He had not told an untruth. It was his strong friendship for Julien which had made him apprehend a duel organized in that way, under the influence of a righteous indignation. Gorka's unjustifiable violence would certainly not permit a second encounter to be avoided. But as the insult had been outrageous, it was the more essential that the conditions should be fixed calmly and after grave consideration. To divert his impatience, Montfanon bade the innkeeper point out to him whither they had carried Florent, and he ascended to the tiny room, where the doctor was dressing the wounded man's leg.

"You see," said the latter, with a smile, "I shall have to limp a little for a month…. And Dorsenne?"

"He is all right, I hope," replied Montfanon, adding, with ill-humor:

"Dorsenne is a fool; that is what Dorsenne is. And Gorka is a wild beast; that is what Gorka is." And he related the episode which had just taken place to the two men, who were so surprised that the doctor, bandage in hand, paused in his work. "And they wish to fight there at once, like redskins. Why not scalp one another?.... And that Cibo and that Pietrapertosa would have consented to the duel if I had not opposed it! Fortunately they lack two seconds, and it is not easy to find in this district two men who can sign an official report, for it is the mode nowadays to have those paltry scraps of paper. One of my friends and myself had two such witnesses at twenty francs apiece. But that was in Paris in 'sixty-two." And he entered upon the recital of the old-time duel, to calm his anxiety, which burst forth again in these words: "It seems they do not decide to separate so quickly. It is not, however, possible that they will fight.... Can we see them from here?" He approached the window, which indeed looked upon the enclosure. The sight which met his eyes caused the excellent man to stammer.... "The miserable men!.... It is monstrous.... They are mad.... They have found seconds.... Whom have they taken?.... Those two huntsmen!.... Ah, my God! My God!".... He could say no more. The doctor had hastened to the window to see what was passing, regardless of the fact that Florent dragged himself thither as well. Did they remain there a few seconds, fifteen minutes or longer? They could never tell, so greatly were they terrified.

As Montfanon had anticipated, the conditions of the duel were terrible. For Pietrapertosa, who seemed to direct the combat, after having measured a space sufficiently long, of about fifty feet, was in the act of tracing in the centre two lines scarcely ten or twelve metres apart.

"They have chosen the duel a 'marche interrompue'," groaned the veteran duellist, whose knowledge of the ground did not deceive him. Dorsenne and Gorka, once placed, face to face, commenced indeed to advance, now raising, now lowering their weapons with the terrible slowness of two adversaries resolved not to miss their mark.

A shot was fired. It was by Boleslas. Dorsenne was unharmed. Several steps had still to be taken in order to reach the limit. He took them, and he paused to aim at his opponent with so evident an intention of killing him that they could distinctly hear Cibo cry:

"Fire! For God's sake, fire!"

Julien pressed the trigger, as if in obedience to that order, incorrect, but too natural to be even noticed. The weapon was discharged, and the three spectators at the window of the bedroom uttered three simultaneous exclamations on seeing Gorka's arm fall and his hand drop the pistol.

"It is nothing," cried the doctor, "but a broken arm."

"The good Lord has been better to us than we deserve," said the Marquis.

"Now, at least, the madman will be quieted…. Brave Dorsenne!" cried Florent, who thought of his brother-in-law and who added gayly, leaning on Montfanon and the doctor in order to reach the couch: "Finish quickly, doctor, they will need you below immediately."

Ingram Content Group UK Ltd.
Milton Keynes UK
UKHW040937140523
421492UK00033B/21